VERMONT

1. Whitingham
2. Heartwellville
3. Ira
4. Thetford
5. Ewells Mill
6. Wallace Pond
7. Albany
8. Swanton
9. Hinesburg
10. East Middlebury
11. Rutland

Warren Kimble

illustrates

THE MARE'S NEST

by

Gary Bowen

HARPERCOLLINSPUBLISHERS

For nearly two years a young artist traveled from one town to the next, crisscrossing the New England states. To everybody who would listen, he read these words from his broadside:

**The remarkable ability
to paint portraits of animals
as they wish to be seen
is my special talent.
Please hire me to create likenesses
of your pets and livestock
today!**

Alas, no one ever bought a painting from this artist. Folks thought it odd that he never made pictures of humans and preferred to paint on pieces of wood rather than canvas.

In the village of Whitingham the artist walked along a road that led to a small farmhouse. There a little girl sat sobbing, holding a dog that began to bark.

"WOOF-achoo-achoo!"

To an average listener the sneezelike sound the pet repeated would have seemed an ordinary "achoo-achoo." But the painter heard the animal exclaim, "It's you, it's you!"

Nearby a farmer waving a hay fork hollered, "Hold it right there! You're that animal artist who stopped here last year." The man came closer, saying, "It was rude when I poked fun at your artwork. Please forgive me. If only I'd let you make a portrait of my daughter's horse, she might not be so sad today."

The painter listened as the farmer explained, "My girl's mare, Morganna, has been missing for more than a month. When the horse was last seen, a whitewasher I hired to paint the barn saw a drifter near our pasture. That stranger likely took Morganna."

Suddenly the dog trembled and whined, "Ite-osh-urr," a sound the artist could not understand.

When the farmer agreed to buy a picture of the child's beloved dog, the painter was elated. "Dreams can come true!" he sang as he began his first commissioned animal portrait.

For the better part of two days the dog posed proudly upon its favorite rug. Once the work of art was completed, the farmer paid the painter generously and asked, "How will you spend your money?"

The artist replied, "My hope is to make paintings of animals like those my grandparents saw when they lived in Africa. As soon as I can afford passage overseas, I'll sail there and one day return to America with scenes of exotic wildlife for all to see!"

Before departing, the artist promised he would come back to paint Morganna's portrait—that is, if the horse came home. The girl gave the painter a copybook, suggesting he tear out a page or two for writing a letter to her, perhaps with news about her missing mare.

JULY 2, 1846

Traveling west, the artist talked to many pet and livestock owners. None were interested in his special talent, but after he told about the child's lost horse, everyone asked him to describe the animal. "The little girl said there are beautiful white spots on the horse's face, she has a very long mane, and she is called Morganna mare."

A well-known horse breeder thought the youngster was probably trying to say she had a Morgan mare, and cautioned, "When you are searching for lost livestock, it helps to know the pedigree." The artist agreed but still felt certain he could recognize the horse on sight.

July 7, 1846

Dear Miss,

Since leaving your home, I walk 15 to 20 miles daily and have traveled to such towns as Bennington, Manchester, Dorset, and Peru. It is sad for me to report that I've had no luck finding your horse.

A woman in Heartwellville is upset too, because all her black-and-white rabbits, with the exception of one named Dutch, vanished just weeks ago. I was paid to paint Dutch's portrait.

The pretty room with the feather bed at your house is a pleasant memory. These days I fashion a lean-to from pine boughs to sleep under.

I remain thankful for having been hired to paint the white dog's portrait.

Best wishes from
Your Artist Friend

July 11, 1846

A dairy farmer in the town of Ira told the artist a sad tale about his Holstein cattle. "Each cow had a special spot on her hide that resembled a New England state, but only Miss Vermont is here now," the farmer moaned. "Don't know what the dickens happened to the others."

Miss Vermont posed for her portrait and mooed, "Marvelous" at the way the painter emphasized her petite head and broad back.

July 20, 1846

On the outskirts of Sharon the artist chatted with a fellow traveler, who lit a fancy white tobacco pipe before saying, "Come fall in Rutland town, a fair is scheduled. You ought to set up a booth there and sell portraits. I've been thinking about painting animals myself, but I'm color-blind. Plans are in the works for a big livestock auction too!" The stranger remounted a dapple-gray mare and started to ride away, shouting, "Hope to see you at the fair!" But the horse stopped, turned to face the painter, and nickered, "Ite-osh-urr?" before trotting along.

The artist felt puzzled: What was the animal trying to tell him?

But he was pleased with the prospect of the Rutland County Fair.

In Thetford village angry residents gathered on the green that was bordered by a white fence. These people, mostly shepherds, shared clues in hopes of capturing the thieves who had made off with their black sheep.

Before mentioning the portrait business, the artist told them about other animals that had mysteriously disappeared.

A woman whispered to the painter, "Those herdsmen are so upset, they cannot appreciate your art—but I do! Follow me." They crossed the street to a house where a fat cat sat patiently. "Poor Pussy looks peaked," the lady said. "I'll feed him soon. How about a picture of Pussy enjoying this wee fellow?" From a sewing basket she pulled out a deer mouse.

Horrified, the artist snapped, "A painting of a cat making a meal of a mouse is not considered art!"

"You'll like this! Watch." The woman placed the tiny critter in front of the hungry cat. Pussy's eyes fixed upon the creature, which made a sound the painter knew was its final *squeak*. The artist lunged at the feline to stop him from devouring the helpless rodent—but missed!

The cat lowered his head toward the mouse until—until their noses touched and Pussy purred and purred! While the mouse licked the cat's whiskers, the lady gave the pair tidbits and said, "Now paint a pretty picture of my two pals!"

AUGUST 3, 1846

Kidnappers took gray goats from Ewells Mill. And it was there that the artist made a double portrait of Morgan horses, for which he was paid a handsome sum.

August 7, 1846

A newspaper reporter in St. Johnsbury told the painter, "It is strange how no white animals have been stolen to date. Next week's headlines should shock subscribers when they read: 'VILLAIN NEVER STEALS *WHITE* LIVESTOCK.'"

The reporter feared that the missing animals had been butchered.

August 19, 1846

In Wallace Pond the artist met a teacher who was touching up paint on a schoolhouse. A fortnight earlier this man's dogs, Samson and Delilah, had gone for recess with some summer school students. Poor Delilah had never returned!

Samson chose an on-guard pose for his portrait. As the dog stood, he frequently whined something that again sounded like "Ite-osh-urr." This strange word continued to confound the artist.

August 31, 1846

Dear Miss,

There is no news of your Morganna's whereabouts. I have made many inquiries, but nothing leads me to your horsie. I will not give up.

Presently I am in Albany, Vermont, where I painted a picture of a woman's new lamb and ewe. The lady claims white animals are less likely to be stolen; therefore she was willing to pay an enormous sum for white sheep to replace the brown ones snatched from her twelve days ago.

Tell your father that there is an invitation to everyone in Vermont state and beyond to attend on September 24 the first Rutland County Fair. Please be there if you are able. I plan to set up a portrait booth.

Give your pa and your pup my best wishes.

Fondly,
Your Artist Friend

September 2, 1846

Sunday morning, August 23, six cygnets in Swanton disappeared. The owner of these young swans claimed, "Human varmints carried them away. No other creature would take just black swans and leave the white ones behind!"

Because fewer and fewer days elapsed between a theft and his learning news of it, the artist believed he was close to the trail of the criminals.

September 8, 1846

In St. Albans the painter boarded a boat on Lake Champlain to sail south to the city of Burlington. The skipper lent him a copy of the local newspaper, which featured these headlines:

STATEWIDE PANIC: ANIMAL OWNERS TERRORIZED
Thieves Must Be Jailed

An item concerning the Rutland County Fair gave details about contests, prizes, and vendor spaces. The event was sixteen days away.

September 13, 1846

A tragedy was suffered by the residents of Hinesburg when red hens disappeared from numerous coops, leaving young chicks as orphans!

September 16, 1846

In East Middlebury a professor told the painter, "My neighbor's black oxen, calico cats, and brown pigs all vanished two nights ago." He added, "It seems you are on the trail of the bandits, but please don't leave without first painting a picture of my new companion. She showed up the night of my retirement party and remains guarding a package that I'm not permitted to touch."

The artist painted while the teacher read aloud from his newspaper. "AUCTION! AUCTION! The widow from Whiteface Farm will sell her late spouse's pure-white breeding stock at the Rutland County Fair."

"Such a herd," the professor declared, "should bring high prices now that everyone wants to own only white livestock."

The painter completed the cat's portrait by sunset and then slept till dawn. When the artist departed, the teacher called out, "You will do well!"

September 21, 1846

After traveling through Sudbury, Brandon, Florence, and Pittsford, the painter arrived in Rutland and was aghast when a woman said, "There's no fair in Rutland this year!" She urged the artist to go tell the "so-called *honorable mayor*" how disappointed he felt.

He did.

"Call me *mayor* if you like—but please don't say 'your honor,'" a young man answered while trying to fit an agitated rooster into a costume.

The painter suggested, "Wouldn't it be kinder to the bird and easier for you to simply display a portrait of the animal wearing that outfit? I could make such a painting if you like."

The rooster crowed in agreement!

"Yes! That's brilliant," the mayor cried. "And after you complete a picture of Rutland's mascot, we'll show it at the biggest fair this county will have ever seen!"

"But sir, I understand there won't be any fair in Rutland."

"That's correct. It was relocated to Castleton, only ten miles away. Exhibitors are setting up there as we speak."

Late into the night, in the mayor's study, the artist painted by the bright light of oil lamps. He worked at an incredible speed, completed the portrait, and then fell asleep on a sofa bed.

SEPTEMBER 22, 1846

The painter was startled awake when the mayor burst into the room shouting, "My rooster missed crowing at daybreak! Where is the bird?"

Both the cage and the rooster had vanished.

His honor dashed off, returning armed with a wooden panel. "Please paint the word REWARD on this board. I'm certain the same outlaws who are stealing animals all over Vermont also swiped my bird."

The painter went to a store and bought materials for assembling his portrait booth. Later the mayor helped load those goods, plus the reward sign, into a horsedrawn wagon, and they set out for Castleton.

Several hours passed before the artist spotted the fairground. The mayor brought the horse to a halt. Awestruck, his honor said, "Look at all these people. This is going to be a fantastic event!"

That evening the mayor slept by a campfire, and the painter recorded some of the day's activities in the copybook until he too dozed off.

September 23, 1846

At dawn his honor awoke and immediately began chatting about the fortune-teller. "When smoke rises from the peak of her tent, I'm to hurry over for a palm reading. What do you think of that?"

The artist cautioned, "Psychics who charge fees misuse their powers." Suddenly the painter's expression changed to horror upon realizing that the leather wallet containing his entire savings was missing! Both the mayor and the artist searched for the money's whereabouts by retracing the painter's steps since they had arrived at the fairground.

"There it is!" his honor shouted, but instead of the artist's wallet, he was pointing at puffs of smoke rising from the fortune-teller's tent. "She's waiting for me!" Off he dashed.

Shortly the mayor returned bubbling with good news about his political future and saying that it was urgent for him to go back to Rutland.

As planned, the painter put up poles to frame his booth and spent the remainder of the day attaching canvas to its sides.

Around six P.M. shouts echoed across the fairground. "The widow from Whiteface Farm is here!" Far in the distance a mammoth white parade appeared, wending its way down the mountain road. Many folks went to lend the lady a hand as well as to inspect her famous white livestock.

Before sundown the artist again searched the area in hopes of finding his lost wallet—but without success. Afterward he went across the fairground to where folks sat near a crackling fire listening to storytellers swap tales until all retired for the night.

8:00 A.M. Upon returning from Rutland, the mayor went to the painter's booth and sang, "You'll be thrilled to see what I found! The psychic said, 'Look near Gookin's mill!'" He unveiled a cage, and inside was the missing rooster, still wearing his patriotic suit. A small group gathered to hear the mascot crow.

"No need of that reward now your bird is back," someone said.

But the mayor offered an idea. "Let's raise a *big* reward for whoever captures the outlaws who keep stealing our pets and livestock!" The crowd cheered. "Anyone with information about missing animals, please write who, what, when, and where in this fellow's copybook." His honor pointed to the painter.

10:30 A.M. A lady told the artist, "That psychic gazed into a crystal ball and saw me buying a big bunny at the auction. I'd like a portrait of the animal, but he can't be brought here. The widow brushed road dust from all her critters, and she intends to keep them pure white for the sale. No one may touch or remove any animal in her corral. Is there some way that you could paint the rabbit's picture?"

"I'll try," the artist said, and he carried his supplies to the Whiteface paddock.

Soon more folks appeared who also wanted portraits of the animals that they too hoped to buy from the widow at the auction.

12:30 P.M. A former town crier bellowed, "At two o'clock judges will name the winners of the best fruits, grains, and vegetables, plus ox pull and sheep contests! A shower is expected, because the cows are lying down."

3:30 P.M. As the artist continued painting, he heard the announcer say, "Judges will award prizes in the following categories: Best Cheese, Maple Sugar, Carpeting, Flannel, and Wool Socks. We're hoping the dark clouds passing over will clear shortly. Our main event is the animal auction beginning at six o'clock."

5:45 P.M. The painter was putting final touches on a cat's portrait when the auctioneer helpers arrived. One said, "Orders are to get the widow's animals under cover before the rain begins." As they rounded up the livestock to lead them across the fairground, an assistant seized the cat, which yowled that perplexing sound—"Ite-osh-urr!"

Alone in the empty paddock, the artist found himself surrounded by all the portraits he had produced since morning. It suddenly occurred to him that his customers might never pay for their pictures if they had no money after the auction. He muttered, "I won't be paid, my wallet will never be found, and I'm not going to Africa. Coming to this fair was a big mistake!"

A thunderbolt struck a peak, illuminated the sky, and rumbled across the valley. The artist quickly transported the paintings to his booth in hopes of protecting them from the weather. The rain began.

5:58 P.M. The painter grabbed his copybook and was hurrying along to the auction when he spied smoke still puffing from the fortune-teller's tent. He stopped and poked his head inside to say, "Madame, I thought you'd want to know that the auction is about to begin."

Through a haze the artist saw the backside of someone who mumbled, "Thanks, I'll tell her"—then dismissed the painter by motioning with a gloved hand that held a white pipe from which all the smoke was rising.

AUCTION BEGINS

6:00 P.M. "Will everyone within the tent squeeze forward so no one stands outside in the dreadful drizzle?" a voice cried. "The man known as the honorable mayor of Rutland would like a few words with us."

Above the applause the mayor was heard saying, "I am not who you think I am." The crowd became silent. "Rutland has no mayor," his honor confessed. An uncomfortable murmur filled the arena.

"Then who are yuh?" was shouted, followed by nervous giggles.

"I'm called 'mayor' by friends who know I wish to run for that office someday—but first, residents of Rutland must decide that we need such an official. The city of Burlington has a mayor, so Rutland ought to as well."

"But your *honor*," someone teased, "you've created a *mare's nest* before you can set in office!"

"No! No!" the would-be mayor said. "Let me explain. A 'mare's nest' refers to a deliberate hoax or a desire to cause confusion. Never was it my intention to do either. I merely accepted the nickname 'mayor' as an honor." The crowd applauded the young politician.

The mayor announced that later he would give a report on the missing animals. He then unfolded a note the artist had handed him earlier and asked the artist to come onstage. His honor read the message aloud. "After the auction everyone who ordered paintings should pay the artist and claim your pictures at the portrait booth." The audience began to laugh—but only because a little girl had climbed onto the stage, tugged the painter's hands, and excitedly gasped, *"Did you spot my Morganna mare?!"* She then led the artist down to the front row, insisting that he sit beside her and her father, the farmer from Whitingham.

A hush came over the crowd as the widow from Whiteface Farm entered. The auctioneer escorted the veiled lady to a chair onstage.

The first animal presented brought the largest sum ever paid in America for a white rabbit. After that, each time the word "sold" was shouted, an even higher price marked a new record sale.

An intermission was called when it became impossible to hear bids above the din of rain beating upon the tent. An attendant carried a pole that had a flat board attached to its end. With this device, he went about pushing against dripping depressions of rainwater collecting on the canvas roof. Each push made a waterfall splash over the outside panels of the tent.

More white chickens, oxen, cats, cows, and pigs were sold!

During another break the mayor read the entries concerning missing pets and livestock recorded in the artist's copybook. He then asked the painter to create a list, beginning with the name of the first town robbed, followed by the second, third, and so on, citing the stolen animals.

As the artist completed the task, the auctioneer said, "Our last critter for sale will be shown shortly." The steady downpour caused so many pockets of water all over the top of the tent that two more fellows with poles went about trying to keep everyone from being dripped upon.

A magnificent white horse was led onto the stage.

"Papa! I want that horsie. Please, Papa, please!"

Whitingham	horse
Heartwellville	rabbits
Ira	cattle
Thetford	sheep
Ewells Mill	goats
Wallace Pond	dog
Albany	sheep
Swanton	cygnets
Hinesburg	hens
East Middlebury	oxen, pigs, cats
Rutland	rooster

The father entered the bidding. As the price soared, bidders dropped out of the auction until only the girl's father and one other person vied to own the animal. With a crack of the gavel the auctioneer shouted, "Sold!" But not to the artist's friends.

Tears filled the child's eyes. Her pa tried to console her, explaining, "She cost too much. Besides, you asked for another dapple-gray horse like Morganna."

"But that can't be," the painter stammered. "The horse you lost was a Morgan mare."

"Oh! No! Her name is Morganna, and she has beautiful white spots on her nose," the little girl sniveled.

"And lots of other white spots all over her *gray* body," the father added, "making her a dapple gray, which is not anything like a Morgan."

For months the artist had been searching for the wrong breed of horse. Speechless, he sat with his head slumped over the copybook and appeared to be reading the list of towns—but his eyes were closed.

A huge curtain, which stretched across the entire stage, lifted to reveal all the animals that had been sold. The crowd cheered the spectacle!

Suddenly the white horse whinnied, *"Ite-osh-urr!"* It did the same again. *"Ite-osh-urr!"* Then the cows joined in, as did chickens, oxen, sheep, and goats. Soon every creature cried, *"Ite-osh-urr! Ite-osh-urr! Ite-osh-urr*! . . ."

When the auctioneer yelled, "Please someone make them be quiet!" the artist's eyes opened and happened to focus on the capital letters beginning the name of each community listed on the page before him. Those letters spelled a word that was amazingly similar to what the livestock were screaming. But the word was not "ite-osh-urr," the painter realized, and then he burst out, "You mean *WHITEWASHER!*" The animals became silent. Everyone was silent. The rain had even stopped.

The widow glared at the artist and snarled, "*Mean whitewasher?* There's no mean *whitewasher* here, you ninny!" She rose, toppling her chair backward, which startled an attendant who had a pole pressed against a deep depression of water left of center stage. *Crack!* The end of the rod slipped and snapped off, leaving a splintered tip that pierced the swollen canvas and released a huge waterfall upon the widow! She skidded on the wet stage and dropped her small bag, from which a crystal ball, some tarot cards, and a white fancy pipe rolled out onto the floor.

"Look, Papa! Her face was painted and she's lost her hair!" All eyes fixed upon the widow's white wig as it floated downstage.

"She's no widow lady," someone shouted. "That's the whitewasher who painted our schoolhouse. I'd recognize that face anywhere!"

"I say it's the fortune-teller!

"No! No! I'm certain that's the painter who whitewashed the fence around our town green, and then we lost our black sheep!"

"And I believe this is the same person who was whitewashing my barn when my little girl's horse, Morganna, disappeared!"

Suddenly the crowd made sounds of amazement as they watched the white horse's color wash away—revealing spots all over her body.

"Papa, it's Morganna! My Morganna mare!"

The artist shouted, "The scoundrel painted the animals white! *Arrest this widow–fortune-teller–whitewasher–thief!*"

As the partially disguised impostor leaped to get away, the artist tackled the culprit to the ground! The villain growled, "This is all a mistake. I know nothing about whitewash!"

Two constables swiftly escorted the criminal to the county jail.

Because it is illegal to sell stolen property, the auctioneer canceled the sale. After the white paint was scrubbed from all the pets and livestock, they were easily identified and eventually reunited with their rightful owners.

Reporters interviewed the painter to prepare their next headlines.

THE DAILY FREE PRESS.

BURLINGTON, VT., FRIDAY EVENING, SEPTEMBER 25, 1846.

Number 1.

Volume 1.

Animal Thief Captured by Itinerant Artist

RUTLAND HERALD.

BY GEO. H. BEAMAN — RUTLAND, FRIDAY, SEPTEMBER 25, 1846. — Vol. 52

Vicious Whitewasher Poses as Widow Fortune-Teller

The Northern Galaxy

MIDDLEBURY, VT.—FRIDAY, SEPT. 25, 1846

VOL. X. NUM.

Empty Barrels of Whitewash Found Hidden near Fairground

Vermont Mercury

PUBLISHED BY HASKELL & PALMER.

VOLUME XI.

WOODSTOCK, VERMONT, FRIDAY, SEPTEMBER 25TH, 1846.

OFFICE AT THE FRANKLIN

Inflating Price Scam Exposed: Equal Values Resume for All Animals!!!

BELLOWS FALLS GAZETTE.

VOL. VIII—NO. 24.

BELLOWS FALLS, VT., FRIDAY, SEPTEMBER 25, 1846.

WHOLE NO.

Artist Gets Big Buck$

At dawn the patriotic rooster crowed daybreak. The artist awoke with a smile upon his face and began dismantling his portrait booth.

The mayor appeared and offered some advice regarding the painter's missing wallet. "Unfortunate events occur in life, and when they do—tell yourself that something good will happen soon! Remember when you lost not only money but also any hope of fulfilling your dreams—but each day brought new possibilities; more paintings sold at the fair, and everyone did pay up. You captured a thief, received a big reward, and now are free to sail to Africa!"

The artist thanked the mayor for his help and said, "There's a promise I must keep before leaving, and that is to paint a portrait of my little friend's horse, Morganna."

And he did.

The Mare's Nest

Library of Congress Cataloging-in-Publication Data
Bowen, Gary.
  The mare's nest / by Gary Bowen ; illustrated by Warren Kimble.
     p.   cm.
  Summary: In nineteenth-century Vermont, an itinerant artist who
travels the New England countryside painting portraits of livestock
and pets discovers a mystery involving some stolen animals.
  ISBN 0-06-028408-0 — ISBN 0-06-028407-2 (lib. bdg.)
  [1. Mystery and detective stories.   2. Painting—Fiction.
3. Animals—Fiction.   4. New England—Fiction.]   I. Kimble,
Warren, ill.   II. Title.
PZ7.B67245 Mar   2001   00-32024
[Fic]—dc21

Typography by Al Cetta
  1 2 3 4 5 6 7 8 9 10

First Edition